Hello Kitty's Family Trip

By Kris Hirschmann
Illustrated by Sachiho Hino

ISBN 978-0-545-45922-8

12 11 10 9 8 7 6 5 4 3 2 1   13 14 15 16/0

Printed in the U.S.A.   40

SCHOLASTIC INC.
New York Toronto London Auckland
Sydney Mexico City New Delhi Hong Kong

🐱 and 🐑 sat in the lunchroom at 🏫. The friends can't wait for spring break!

🐑 and her family were going to the 🌊. 🐱 and her family were going camping. 🐑 wanted to know if 🐱 could visit her at the 🌊.

🐱 didn't think so. Her family would be too far away.

🐑 would miss 🐱 very much.

🐱 hugged her friend and promised to write her lots of ✉️. She would give 🐑 all of the ✉️ when 🏫 started again.

🐑 promised to do the same. She would think about 🐱 every day.

🐱 packed for her trip. She filled half of her 👜 with 👕. She filled the other half with 📓 and ✏️. 🐱 looked at her full 👜. She thought about all the ✉️ she would write.

🐱 and her family drove to the campground the next morning. 🐱 wanted to write to 🐑 during the drive. But then she saw a 🌳 covered with tiny green 🌿. She pointed out the spring 🌿 to her sister, 🐱.

🐱 spent the rest of the drive looking out her 🪟.

set up her ⛺. Then she got out her 🔲 and ✏️.

She got ready to write to 🐑.

🐱 heard a sound outside her ⛺.

It was a family of 🐣. Seven baby 🐣 waddled behind their mother.

🐱 thought they were so sweet!

She leaped up and followed the 🐣.

🐱 forgot all about writing ✉️.

(Hello Kitty) woke up early the next morning.

She decided to write to (Mama) today.

But she didn't have time. (Papa) and (Grandpa) took (Kitty) and (Mimmy) on a (picnic)

in a grassy ███ .

(Kitty) ate, played with (Mimmy), and enjoyed the spring (sun) on her face.

🐱 glanced at her 📓 and ✏️ the next day. She should write to 🐑.

But it was such a nice day. She invited 🐱 to go pick 🌸.

They ran to a nearby ▢.

🐱 and 🐱 picked 🌸 all day long.

They had a great time.

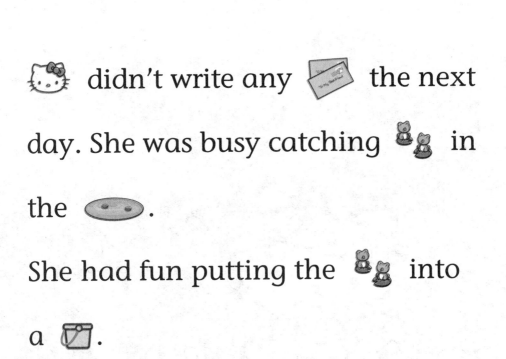 didn't write any the next day. She was busy catching in the .

She had fun putting the into a .

The days flew by. Soon it was time to pack up and go home.

picked up her . She opened her . There she saw all of her unused .

felt terrible about not writing to .

was afraid to see at

the next day.

Would be upset?

walked over to her friend.

was so sorry. She had a fun time

at the . But she forgot to write

any . wanted to know

if was mad at her.

🐱 wasn't mad. 🐑 was her best friend. Besides, 🐱 forgot to write, too!

🐱 and 🐑 both had fun and the best spring break ever.

Did you spot all the picture clues in this Hello Kitty book?

Each picture clue is on a flash card. Ask a grown-up to cut out the flash cards. Then try reading the words on the backs of the cards. The pictures will be your clue.

Reading is fun with Hello Kitty!

beach	Hello Kitty®
letters	Fifi
bag	school

Mama	window
Papa	tent
picnic	ducks

tree	clothes
leaves	paper
Mimmy	pencils

frogs	meadow
pond	sun
pail	flowers